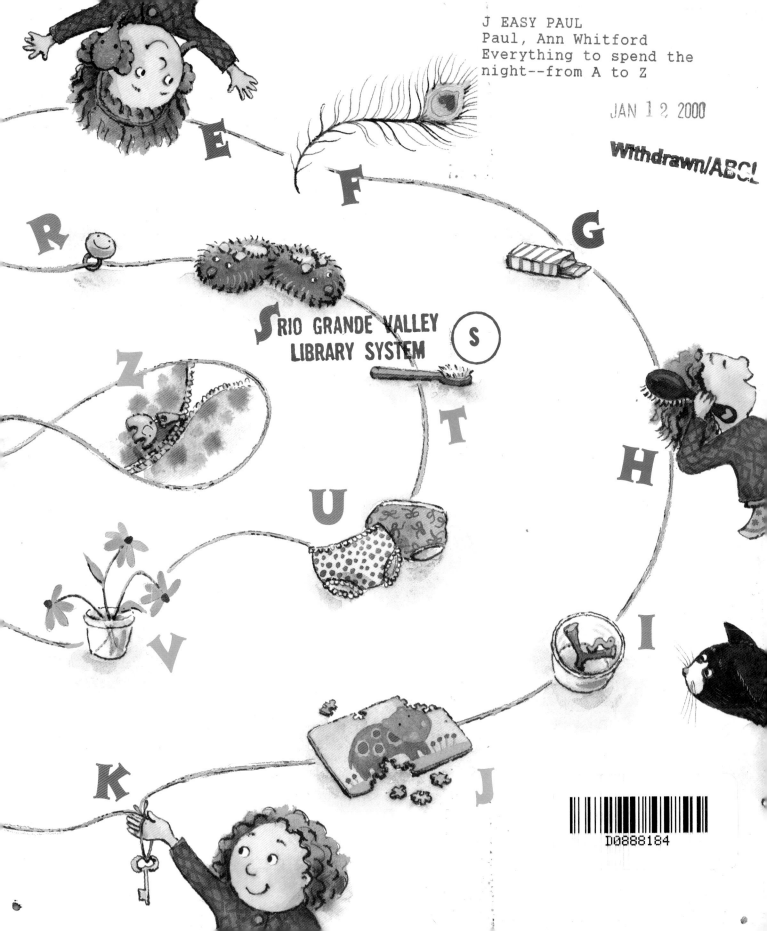

RIO GRANDE VALLEY
LIBRARY SYSTEM

For the Write Sisters, my wonderful sleep-over friends. —A.W.P.

For Becky. —M.S.

EVERYTHING TO SPEND THE NIGHT

FROM
A TO Z

A Melanie Kroupa Book

A Melanie Kroupa Book

**DK
Ink**

DK Publishing, Inc.
95 Madison Avenue
New York, New York 10016

Visit us on the World Wide Web at http://www.dk.com

Text copyright © 1999 Ann Whitford Paul   Illustrations copyright © 1999 Maggie Smith

Library of Congress Cataloging-in-Publication Data
Paul, Ann Whitford.
    Everything to spend the night from A to Z / by Ann Whitford Paul; illustrated by
Maggie Smith. — 1st ed.
            p.   cm.
    "A Melanie Kroupa book."
    Summary: While showing her grandfather all the things, from A to Z, that she has brought
with her to spend the night, a little girl suddenly realizes she forgot one important item.
    ISBN 0-7894-2511-4
    [1. Grandfathers—Fiction. 2. Bedtime—Fiction. 3. Alphabet. 4. Stories in rhyme.]
I. Smith, Maggie [date], ill. II. Title.
PZ8.3.P273645Ev   1998   97-43593
[E]—dc21   CIP
                                                                  AC

Book design by Chris Hammill Paul. The text of this book is set in 19 point Horley Old Style.
The illustrations for this book were painted in watercolor.

Printed and bound in the United States of America

First Edition, 1999

10 9 8 7 6 5 4 3 2

Grandpa! Grandpa!

Come and see
the things I brought
for you and me—
I packed my bag.
I filled it tight with . . .

EVERYTHING TO

I ♥ Dogs

A DK INK BOOK

DK PUBLISHING, INC.

SPEND THE NIGHT

words by Ann Whitford Paul

pictures by Maggie Smith

First some **A**pples we can share
with **B**unny and my fuzzy **B**ear.

They cry whenever I'm not home.
I couldn't leave them all alone.

And look! A box of yellow **C**halk.

Can we play hopscotch
on the walk?

Silly cat! You can't stay
on number four.
You're in our way.

I hit my **D**rum.

I BANG and POUND.

Step high, Grandpa!
March around.

Am I too loud?
Look in here—

I brought **E**armuffs
for your ears.

Lie way back.
Close your eyes—
squeeze them tight
for my surprise.

A **F**eather!
Tickle on your chin.

Open wide.
I pop **G**um in.

And now a **H**airbrush
for your hair.

Oops!
Sorry, Grandpa—
nothing's there.

Inside this jar's a green **I**nchworm. Watch it wiggle. Watch it squirm.

Come on, Grandpa. Help me do . . .

my **J**igsaw puzzle—just us two.

Are you ready for the best?

This **K**ey is to my treasure chest.

Turn the **L**ock. Coins to eat!

Now it's time for dancing feet.

My **M**usic box will play the song.

Let's *twirl* and spin

and sing along.

I'm not tired, Grandpa. See!
I packed more
things for you
and me.

I need this **N**ight-light
in my room.

It glows just like a chunk of moon.

Now let's pretend we're in a lake.

I brought an **O**ar.

Watch me take two chairs,

add **P**illows. . . .

Look, a boat!

Climb on board. Off we float.

Here's my **Q**uilt.
I drape it down
and cut gold paper
into crowns.

Ta-daaaaaa!

I'm Queen . . .

. . .and you're my king.

I even brought a royal **R**ing,

and royal **S**lippers, soft as fleece,

a royal **T**oothbrush for my teeth,

plus lots of royal **U**nderwear—my favorite polka-dotted pair!

A gift for you: my queen's bouquet.

This jar's a **V**ase where it can stay.

No, Grandpa, please—
it's not too late.
This won't take long.
I promise. Wait.

I wave my **W**and. I disappear.

Find me!

Find me!

Over here!

Just one more game? I brought my jacks.

Toss the **X**s. Cat, stay back.

This ball of **Y**arn is yours to chase.
Have fun with it some other place.

Now I zip the **Z**ipper tight.

That's *everything* to spend the night.

Time for bed?
But I'm not sleepy.
You didn't see *me* yawn.

Allll riiiiiight,
I'll put my pj's on.

Oh, no!

Where are they?

What can I do?

Yours fit me, Grandpa!

I love you.